D1738881

Tenderness

Other books of poetry by Joyce Carol Oates

Anonymous Sins and Other Poems (1969)
Love and Its Derangements (1970)
Angel Fire (1973)
The Fabulous Beasts (1975)
Women Whose Lives Are Food,
    Men Whose Lives Are Money (1978)
Invisible Woman: New & Selected Poems 1970–1982 (1982)
The Time Traveler (1989)

TENDERNESS

Joyce Carol Oates

Ontario Review Press + Princeton

The Ontario Review Press
9 Honey Brook Drive
Princeton, NJ 08540

Distributed by George Braziller, Inc.
171 Madison Avenue
New York, NY 10016

Library of Congress Cataloging-in-Publication Data

Oates, Joyce Carol, 1938–
Tenderness / Joyce Carol Oates
I. Title
PS3565.A8T44 1996   811'.54—dc20   96-1726
ISBN 0-86538-085-6

First Edition

ACKNOWLEDGEMENTS

The poems in this volume have originally appeared, often in slightly different versions, in the following magazines. My thanks to the editors involved.

AGNI REVIEW, "O Crayola!," "The Bullfrogs," "The Thin Rain"
ATLANTIC MONTHLY, "$"
BOULEVARD, "Rise Up, O Men of God," "Summer Squall," "Old Concord Cemetery," "Off-Season," "Frequent Flier I," "Frequent Flier II," "He Was Talking About His Friend," "In Blue Nantucket"
CHELSEA, "Flash Flood," "In the Country of the Blue," "Hermit Crab"
DOUBLETAKE, "Tenderness"
FOUR QUARTERS, "Recurring Dream of Childhood"
GETTYSBURG REVIEW, "Orion"
HUDSON REVIEW, "What Is Most American Is Most in Motion"
KENYON REVIEW, " The Triumph of Gravity"
MALAHAT REVIEW, "Child Walking in Sleep"
MICHIGAN QUARTERLY REVIEW, "Upstairs"
THE NATION, "Snapshot Album"
NEW LETTERS, "The Infant's Wake"
NEW MYTHS/MSS, "Marsena Sportsman's Club, 1957"
NEW REPUBLIC, "On this Morning of Grief," "The Lord Is My Shepherd"
NEW YORKER, "Flirtation," "Recollection, in Tranquility," "Nostalgia"
PARIS REVIEW, "Prenatal," "Like Walking to the Drugstore, When I Get Out," "Immobility Defense"
POETRY, "Burning Oak, November," "Motive, Metaphor"
PRAIRIE SCHOONER, "Once Upon a Time"
SALMAGUNDI, "Elegy: The Ancestors," "Dakota Mystery, 10 May 1994," "Undertow, Wolf's Head Lake," "The Insomniac"
SEWANEE REVIEW, "The Riddle"
TRIQUARTERLY, "Ballad of Ashfield Avenue"
VIRGINIA QUARTERLY REVIEW, "Island, 1949," "Lost Creek," "The Stone Well," "Insomnia"
WESTERN HUMANITIES REVIEW, "The Black Glove," "Hands, Prints, Time: A Collage," "There Was a Shot"
YALE REVIEW, "Sexy"

"O Crayola!" and "Such Beauty!" were printed in limited editions by William B. Ewert, Concord, New Hampshire.

For my husband, Raymond

CONTENTS

I
Tenderness

O Crayola!

—for John Updike

Shall we tell them thanks but why
reward us who, as children,
filled in time by filling in
coloring books? Or shall we lie?

O Crayola!—even the taste was good.

Glimpsed from a Car, Quickly Passing

—for Henry Bienen

Clothes on that line, headless
in the chill May wind but such antics!
such a mad happy dance of legs, arms!
torsos male-muscled in wind!
and tulip-bright colors,
streaked checked solid plaid!

Let's set our clocks to zero
and begin the universe again!

In the chill May wind.

In Blue Nantucket

In blue Nantucket
half the sea is sky.

In bright September,
that northeast knell.

White-throated waves
in insatiable abundance!

We were so happy here.
What's a family but memories?
Now I dream the ocean is a throat.

History is washed away,
washed under and returns in Roman script
on perfect ribbons of sand,
unreadable.

No night so black as these clamorous waters.
No day so blinding-brilliant.
Scintilla of waves!
Nowhere to hide.

In blue Nantucket,
half the sky is sea.

It's been a sort of race,
which of us can forget more,
more quickly.

High Palladian clouds,
in blue Nantucket.
Clarity of washed glass.
Tracery of white-throated gulls.
Beauty?—a matter of distance.

All time is now,
in blue Nantucket.

Eelgrass, arrowwood, bayberry.
Strange horizontal planes of moors.
Mists like brooding thought,
        the sour odor of unacted desire.

I've come to hate my own hypocrisy,
accepting sympathy for the wrong griefs.

Secret pleasure of loss, and of hurt.
The wild rose that grows everywhere on the island,
        insatiable. The briars.
Beach plums red-tumescent by mid-September.
When lightning laces the air,
in blue Nantucket.

She told me, 'You forgive too easily.
You're cheap.'

In blue Nantucket, that ceaseless wind.

In blue Nantucket, swarm of shrieking gulls,
        all eyes, beaks, appetite.

Footprints at the water's edge, bare feet
and each toe defined, yet how swiftly
        filling in, with froth.
In blue Nantucket.

Flirtation, July 1953

Driving north a day and a half from Pensacola, Florida.
My father young, flat-bellied, impatient behind the wheel.
Now in his civvies, khaki shorts and T-shirt.
My mother and five-month baby brother in the back seat
    of the Chevy.
Long hours of driving, windows rolled down to cascades
    of bright steamy air.
Now it's night but still warm, humid as an exhaled breath.
A bone-blind moon in the sky hurting my eyes.
In Kentucky, at the edge of a nameless town, an Esso station
    and a café. Moths swirling crazy in the light, thick
    as snowflakes.
Dazed with sleep. Eyelashes stuck together. My neck is too
    weak for me to raise my head from the sticky vinyl back
    of the seat.
My mother has taken the baby into the women's restroom
    to change his soaked diaper.
My father is in the café drinking milk, three, four tall brimming
    glasses of cold milk, he's still in training.
(Though he lost the big, title fight, light-heavyweight division
    U.S. Army, last week. We weren't allowed to attend, he'd
    said we'd jinx him but that's another story.)
It's the smell of gasoline that wakes me.
And the garage attendant squirting liquid onto the windshield.
Then with a soiled rag he rubs away the splattered insects
    in rough erratic circles leaving an oily-iridescent gleam.
Heavy-muscular guy about my father's age, maybe younger.
A face deep-stained like a football. Black sideburns curling
    onto his cheeks. Droopy-eyed.
He slides into the driver's seat stinking of sweat, grease,
    gasoline, he's testing the windshield wipers, then the turn
    signals.
Impressed with the Chevy, a 1952 model. How's one of these
    hold the road? he asks.
Wearing a dirt-stiffened Esso uniform, on top a metal-studded
    leather vest and his biceps are bunchy as an adult woman's
    breasts, and tattooed.

7

Gripping the steering wheel like he's driving in my father's
    place.
Saying words I can't understand at first, it's the nasal-drawl
    sweet-Southern accent I'd almost think was put on to
    make me laugh. And I *do* laugh, shivery breathy giggle.
Poking me, a forefinger in the collarbone, Sleepyhead?
Asking me, Where you folks goin?
I tell him Buffalo.
Buf'lo—what?
Buffalo, New York.
You comin from Flor'da?
I tell him yes, now my daddy's discharged from the U.S. Army
    where he'd been a corporal and now going home.
He been in the War? K'rea?
Yes, I say. My voice is proud. Didn't get wounded, either.
I'm twelve years old. A thin girl, flat-chested, bony wrists he
    could circle with thumb and forefinger.
Tiny grit-hard pimples across my forehead beneath my bangs
    stinging like red pepper.
My brown hair is pulled back into a greasy ponytail, secured
    by a rubber band my mother's deft fingers twisted.
I'm in wrinkled shorts, pullover terrycloth blouse, rubber-thong
    sandals out of a bin at Woolworth's.
I'm sweaty too so I keep my fuzzy underarms shut tight.
He's saying, leaning close, You're cute, hon, how old are you?—
    and I'm staring with this grin, frozen scared.
He's saying in this low-drawling voice he wouldn't want
    anybody to overhear if there was anybody close enough
    to overhear which there isn't, Hey y'know?—hon?—you got
    one of them flying roaches on you,—brushing the front of my
    blouse, gently, the back of his oil-smeared hand,—five-inch
    roach the kind that *bites.* Uh-oh!
But it's only a joke, he's laughing.
Front seat of the Chevy rocking with his laughing.

That was the first. You never forget your first.

The Thin Rain

This still ripe heart of summer, such
nights when everyone you love is sleep-
ing, or gone.

When you were a child the sky darkened
to unreadable constellations. There,
all is mute. And here

your eyes are flat as coins
reflecting light, not giving.
You can't name the precise sin

for which you've been doing penance
but this is what living requires:
not naming what has screwed itself, shrewd

tiny knot, into your heart. As when
you were a child and adults wept inconsolable
behind shut doors while grief washed
lightly about you like summer rain

thinning as it falls.

Nightmare, So Sweet

Light as froth you lie on the coarse
cottony surface of the sea. That's the wisest
strategy.

Distant steeples?—steadfast lighthouse lights?
And a thin sickle moon mute
as art? O the good that surrounds us.
They are there but you are here

where by slow degrees the thing
squeezes out of your plump plum
of a heart. Eye arterial red. Genitalia
bunched like fruit. Squatting

on your chest: that classic pose.
If someone sleeps beside you he'd have
difficulty recalling your name, now.
Or whether that face, so exposed,
is one he knows.

The Bullfrogs

At dusk the bullfrogs begin
Singly & shyly at first
hidden in tall grasses at the edge
of our pond   hidden in night
in the earth's moist bowels
what deep guttural calls
what somber reptilian lust
belly-croaks   bulging eyes
pleas promises & demands
Love   love love me only
me

And you others, men no longer young
gone slack in the gut, pouchy jowls
& hair thinning slantwise combed
over strange domes of heads—
What is this? what has happened?
Will you love me just the same?
Me only me only   me?

Boys' eyes & clumsy groping hands
we grip. *Well, yes.*

Off-Season

This afternoon after the storm the Atlantic sky is black-
blowing and the beach is crazed with wind, surf
choppy like jeering laughter. I'm in a place I've
never been of empty stalls, row upon row in a women's
changing shed and all empty, everyone gone
home, doors slamming in the wind. And something
sly as a snake swimming in the rippled sand beneath
the floorboards too quick to be seen—.

How many years pass leaving us unchanged, and
the sky's terrible silence unchanged. The pounding
of the surf that is the same surf you heard when
you were eleven, or fourteen, this sharp smell
of damp wood and damp concrete and disinfectant and
dried urine and a melancholy you can taste, delicious
on the tongue as tears, or the sea. *Hello!* I cry,
Where are you hiding! and there's nothing
except in a corner in a jumble of old wrappers
cigarette butts broken lipsticks and combs, the dime-
store bracelet lost, or stolen, how many years ago
and now I stand here turning it in my fingers,
an oily feel to the cheap metal, it weighs nothing
and it's tarnished and there's a stranger's name
engraved on the plate, why then so happy and why
so suddenly in a corner of an empty changing shed
in the off-season of a year nearly gone—.

How we return to what we haven't known we've lost.

On This Morning of Grief

Cupped in your hands you bring me
an abandoned wrens' nest—
exquisite in miniature
the fine-woven grasses like silk,
moss that's still green,
soiled string, milkweed seed, white cat fur—
and in the precise center a hollow
and in the hollow a single eggshell
from which life
has pecked its way free, and flown:
smaller than my smallest fingernail,
delicately brown-speckled—
the egg's halves parted
like an eye on the verge of opening.

Once Upon a Time

November, season of heartbreak. Riding
the white-painted strip from Manhattan to
New Brunswick. Skeins of sleety rain falling,
lifting. Overhead lights wink like mad planets.
You've been here before, rolling southward
in a spell of gravity, banking the turns,
the infinite curves,
I wish—I wish!—we might live forever:
the night tide of Jersey, the smell beyond
sweetness, smokestacks regal and deathly
as bloodied hair.

Where fish flash silver it's broken glass,
puddles bright as tongues, the thistle field
where the abductor finally strangled the child, and
God's voices—these soiled birds flung
against the windshield. I wish I knew
to love the strangers in the oncoming headlights,
this glitter of traffic
following us into the next world.
And now a wall of night punctuated by lights
as sleep by dreams—

No Savior came this way
more than once.

Sexy

His name was Eddy S. Drove an electric-blue Buick convertible.
Fish-fins, white walls. Bright-glaring chrome
pocked in rust like acne.
Speeding down the long slope of Rt. 78
south of Lake Ontario.
Restless Eddy S., always in a hurry.
Eddy S. the dangerous one.
Dreamy-hooded eyes, a gaze
like hot brown syrup pouring over us.
And his hair we'd memorized:
stiff-rippled, vaseline-slick, color of tarnished brass.
Pompadour erect as a rooster's comb.
Every other word Eddy S. and his friends uttered was filth.
Or boyish-grinning *hell! shit! damn! God-damn!*
They were their fathers' sons.
Graduated high school, or quit, or expelled—
working now on construction, as garage mechanics,
one of them, not Eddy, a plumber's assistant.
Those sharky discolored teeth!—Eddy S.'s slow smile.
Oh Eddy S., you had our hearts.
We were scared of you.
Vying for your fleeting attention, your eyes
flicking toward us, and away,
headlights out of the night flaring up,
rushing past,
blinding,
and gone.

You have to understand: this was 1959.
That world. And everyone then
is dead now.
Or it's the same thing.
Eddy S. might've impregnated that girl from Akron
and if so if she had his baby that baby would be thirty-five now.
Eddy S. chain-smoking Camels, drinking beer, fidgety
when he wasn't in his car, scratching his lean stomach

through his T-shirt. Brassy-kinky hairs on his arms,
an American flag tattoo on his right forearm.
Gunning the Buick's motor, throwing gravel in his wake.
Nineteen years old when it happened.
I remember: wind darkening the sky above Lake Ontario.
One minute there's sun, the next there's a sky of clouds.
There's a way the Olcott Beach ferris wheel looked
when the sky changed. Giddy rotating lights
against the storm-black sky before the first raindrops
are blown like buckshot.
Eddy S., I wonder did you ever pause to see?
smell that air charged like electricity before a storm?
Or were you already pulling out of the parking lot,
beside you a girl's blond-streaked hair whipping in the wind—
and no looking back?

Three times I rode in Eddy S.'s crazed Buick.
Not alone. Jammed in the rear with my friends,
and two others jammed in front with Eddy S.
speeding along the highway.
Convertible top down, radio blaring
and wind blinding as a cataract.
Eddy S. with his bottle of Molson's locked between his knees.
Eddy S. driving wild, swerving to avoid a pick-up truck
and we screamed,
and clutched at one another,
and laughed till we were weak.
Laughed till our bladders ached.
Laughed till tears stung our cheeks.
Then that zigzag move—Eddy S. steering the Buick over
the train tracks at Ransomville,
as the crossing gates lowered,
red danger lights flashing.
Oh Eddy S., you had our hearts,
we would've died for you.

Sexy we whispered of Eddy S.
Sexy was a word you didn't say aloud.
Like *sex, sexual* never aloud, nor to any adult.

16

We thought Eddy S. was *sexy*, which was why
our girls' knees turned to water in his presence.
Our hearts were fluttering birds inside our ribcages.
Sexy Eddy S. but it was his seed needing to burst forth.
Hot and compressed as shot needing to be discharged.
Or coin-sized phlegm on the tongue needing to be spat out.
In any moist fleshy crevice, any girl's pouch.
Back seat of the Buick, the frayed vinyl cover.
The rumors we'd heard!
The girl from Akron, another girl from Depew.
Girls without names clustering around him and his friends
at Olcott Beach. Where once
below the boardwalk Eddy S. kissed me.
We'd been fooling around, flirting.
Eddy S.'s breath beery-sour, a cigarette in his fingers
he'd offered me to take a puff of, *C'mon, try.*
So I did, coughing.
Grabbing me then and pressing against me
like I'd dreamed he would except
I went rigid in terror so scared
I could not breathe.
Asking me then how'd I like to come for a ride?
Hot balmy August evening, the floodlit water tower OLCOTT
     BEACH.
Ferris wheel, roller coaster, merry-go-round lights,
hurdy-gurdy music. Sickish-sweet odor of cotton candy,
pickle relish. Discarded hotdog buns buzzing flies.
I panicked at Eddy S.'s touch and backed away.
He'd been drinking, sure he was drunk, sure
another girl he'd preferred wasn't at the beach tonight.
Sure he was pissed off, hot-syrupy eyes angry now,
not quite in focus.
Like a big upright doll somebody's shaken so hard
the eyes won't ever match again.
Sexy Eddy S. God's purest seed-
deliverer, babymaker-machine.
His loins, his hips, his cock
hidden behind the glinting zipper
where you must not look,

17

and I did not.
You didn't think of any of the guys that way.
That's the trick of it—you don't think.
Like I wasn't thinking I was scared to ride in Eddy S.'s Buick
because I was scared of dying in a drunken crash
because I never thought of dying.
It was a movie I hadn't seen, not even the coming attractions.
I was scared of Eddy S.'s angry eyes. Hard hands
that could hurt, the mouth in that grin that wasn't so sweet.
Groin bulging hard against my belly when he'd grabbed me,
fingers hurting my shoulders.
I wore my pink-puckered swimsuit, a terrycloth shirt over it.
I was scared of what Eddy S. would ask of me,
what he'd do to me in his car parked above the lake.
"Blue Ontario's shore"—
my life might have been changed.
Impregnated in sixty seconds, back seat of Eddy S.'s Buick,
tepid waves lapping below on the beach,
that faint fish-odor, decaying clams.

Sexy we whispered of Eddy S. His oiled hair,
duck's-ass cut, tight jeans and T-shirt,
his flag-tattooed right arm.
In his swim trunks, muscled legs covered in brassy fuzz,
thighs lean and flat as boards.
Eddy S. and his friends hot like rabbits to procreate their kind.
Hot like buzzing flies, like gulls. Like dogs mating
as if a magnetic force has slammed them together moaning
and yipping. What pulsing need we can't name,
unspeakable gravity of need.
Wanting to make babies, make babies, make babies
until every crevice, every fissure, every orifice of Earth
is jammed with human flesh.
I want you, I need you, I'm crazy for you Oh Baby.
Eddy S. careless in his shooting seed as the beer bottles
the guys tossed from their speeding cars.
And not a glance back, why take the time?—no time.
We're in a hurry to get where we are going.
I was scared of what Eddy S. would do or try to do in his car

and what might happen to me if he was thwarted doing it.
Thirteen that summer, and already I knew
you don't provoke them.
Don't lead a guy on especially not an older guy
especially not one who's been drinking.
You respected them, that need in them, the anger in the need.
Like you respected the undertow off the pier
that could sweep you away out of warm lapping daylit water.
Drown you in a frenzy of black churning cold
in five minutes.
But I said no, or tried to.
Panicked backing away.
It scared me, the panting heat of a stranger's breath,
facial skin close-up stippled with pimples.
Teeth the color of beer. And dirt-edged nails
and hands just clumsy enough, and rough,
showing he's scared, too, in his different way.
I backed away from Eddy S. so scared
I knew he could see my heart pounding palpitating
my tiny breasts. And he stared at me in contempt,
dismissal. Running his hands swiftly through his oiled hair,
curling his lip like Elvis. *So?—go.*
I ran up the steps to the boardwalk, which was crowded.
Astonished no one seemed to know, nor even to glance at me.
My shaking hands, excited eyes.
A thick-clouded sky at dusk, red sun at the hazy lake horizon
like blood draining, and darkness coming from the east.
And the ferris wheel turning, squeals and drunken music.
Lights rotating, lights encircling lights.
Only a memory.
Not even a snapshot.
You'd think all this would be lost in time.
But Eddy S. is more real to me
than any of you.

Though Eddy S. has been dead for thirty-five years.
Boxed the guys said, crude word to disguise their loss.
Boxed and gone under the hill, a Lutheran cemetery
near Olcott I never visited.

Eddy S. with one of his girls drunk-driving one Saturday night
after Labor Day, speeding on Rt. 78 up from Mt. Ephraim.
Eighty-five miles an hour they estimated from the skid marks.
He'd hit the brakes and the Buick fishtailed and he'd gone
through a guard rail down a steep incline below the fairgrounds.
Eddy S.'s head plunged through the Buick's windshield.
Eddy S.'s lean body was smashed like plywood.
And the streaked-blond girl from Ransomville none of us knew—
a leg severed from her body. Body thrown thirty feet.
How death took them up, shook and tossed them like dice.
That's how easy it is?
And in the *Olcott Journal,* their twinned photographs.
So they seemed in death a couple.
So they seemed in death destined for each other
or destined anyway for this
though what name to give to this?—
none of us knew.

My girl friend Janet's bitter-twisting mouth—
"What did he see in *her*?"

Tenderness

In the Pennysaver Food Mart, 6:40 P.M. of a rain-darkened
    Tuesday.
The aisles near-empty, bright-glaring as TV.
A sad-eyed guy the downside of forty, brown corduroy jacket,
    dark tieless shirt, shopping alone.
Slow as a man in a dream, pushing a cart with one wheel
    sticking.
That vague dazed drowning-fish look of the solitary male
    adrift in unknown territory women navigate with craft,
    quick eyes.

Please! out of my way!—I'm able to avoid him until in Fresh
    Produce there he is blocking the aisle. Staring
    at picked-over lettuce, limp green beans.
Those pulpy "vine-ripened" tomatoes I'd warn him against
    if he was my problem, and he isn't.
I'm noting his Brillo-kinky graying hair damp-combed
    over a bulb of a head.
Hovering shadow of a beard. Hasn't shaved since 7 A.M.
Eyes like hesitant minnows behind tinted glasses.
I'm noting the L.L. Bean jacket of zipper pockets, vestigial
    buckles and belts.
Water-stained old running shoes.
Six-feet-two, sinewy-lean. Slightly rounded shoulders.
Used to play basketball once, or touch football.
Now going to fat at the waist where it doesn't show, yet,
    inside his clothes.
Could be a high school teacher, math. An accountant.
Something in computers?
Divorced and lost custody of the kids except for weekends.
Divorced and lost his way.
Or his wife's sick, really sick, the first time ever
    and he's scared.
Or he's never married, and just moved here—
    his mother died, he's been transferred.

That look in his face *Where is this?* glimpsed above a pyramid
    of California melons, the tasteless kind, and expensive.
That crinkled face *Why?* wondering *Is it too late for me?*
And the damned cart wheel sticking.

By Aisle 3, pickles, relish, mustard, cheap glittering "glass-
    ware" I've forgotten him.
By Aisle 4, rice, pasta, "gourmet & ethnic foods,"
    I'm moving fast.
Except in Aisle 5 there he is, again blocking my way.
Searching the shelves for God knows what: Rice Krispies?
    Drano? Kleen Kitty Litter? Welch's Hawaiian Punch?
Excuse me! a woman shopper pushes past him.
Now seeing he's blocking my way he pushes his cart clumsily
    into a stack of Campbell's soup boxes unpacked in the aisle.
Our eyes don't meet, I'm already past.
Look, why should I smile. I'm in a hurry.
I don't make eye contact with strangers. I'm in a hurry.
One of those who knows this store blind.
What she wants, and where it is. Or maybe.
What she wants that can be bought.

Food Mart dreams!—I used to have them, dreamy-eyed amid
    the cans, packages, Muzak that's always "I'm Dreaming of a
    White Christmas."
Dew-eyed navigating the aisles, turn a corner and there's
    my fate?
Not now. We're talking years later.
Not now. I'm exhausted from a long day of whatever it is
    our days are.
American, discount-priced, guaranteed plastic.
I'm exhausted from dreaming in the interstices of a life.
Those subterranean stories we invent where we're central
    to whatever it is out there surrounding us.
Those stories insisting we're important, anyway we're *here*.
And in my cart I'm dropping a package of paper towels.
A box of "floral embossed" paper napkins.

On tiptoe reaching for a box of yellow Kleenex ("unscented")
        so tenuously balanced atop a stack of boxes
        the slightest imbalance will knock everything down.
I'm not tall enough, I can't reach the box.
This is my life! I can't reach the box!
A sob of frustration, a hurt in the heart. You know that hurt!
And suddenly from behind, unannounced the man in the
        corduroy jacket reaches out to take the box of Kleenex,
        fingers light and deft, and hands it to me.

I murmur "Thanks!" my face burning.
He's already past, pushing his lopsided cart.

What sweet acts of tenderness, anonymous.
In the Pennysaver Food Mart, rain-darkened Tuesday.

II
Undertow

Prenatal

Here is the wide veranda striped in sunshine
and here, beside the house, those bushes heavy
with tiny white clustered berries said
to be poison though burst against the tongue

they have no taste, or nearly. Here,
the oak bannister and the dizzy ascendancy
of stairs. The toilet bowl ringed with rust.
The sobbing behind a locked door. And here,

though you won't want to look, the tide
of black ants in the cupboard, the beetles
roiling in the earthen cellar. Black winter rain
dripping from the shingled roof,

the giddy heat of May for which no one is
prepared, and the constellations in their slow
plunge across the sky.... How many millennia
have not known us!

The baby carriage, leathery black like a bat's wings,
waits on the veranda, and here, in the doorway,
hat pushed forward on his blunt young head, hand
raised smartly in greeting, your father.

How many millennia.

Island, 1949

Walking the crude rock
        dam above the
rapids. Why are you
        doing it?—
you might fall,
        drown,

arms useless
        as wings.
You can't turn back,
        others are
watching. And
        such slow

water above the dam
        like thin sleep-
ing mud.
        That summer smell.
Sun-bleached rock,
        duckweed in

clots. Dead bull-
        heads,
clams. Waste
        from outhouses up-
stream and you've been
        warned but

you can't turn back
        and when you step
on the island it's
        nothing of course—
a single scrub willow,
        roots exposed,

dying. And that stink.
    And broken glass.
And your eyes seared
    from sun.
And across the rapids
    your five-year-old brother

wading staring
    and the others call-
ing scornful
    of all you've dared
and how small the island
    and

the other bank so far away,
    looking new, altered,
like a dream you can't
    recall.
And you knew going back
    was more than
you could do.
You knew.

Lost Creek

That shallow fast-running
    creek. White
rapids. The mud-colored
    water breaking
in anger brittle as
    bone.

You can't see where
    it comes from
or where it is going
    in such anger
and how
    could you stop

once you've fallen
    and are being
carried away by the current
    choking, tumbling, rock-
bruised
    and helpless

drowning for miles
    downstream
where no one will know
    your name,
or face.
    Like the girl

who'd drowned they said
    up in Innisfail
or was it she'd been
    beaten and thrown
into the creek so the story
    was Death but more

than Death and no one
        would tell you.
Not even her name.
        Though many times
you saw her in the crazed
        rapids white

arms flailing like
        your own,
hair drenched down
        her back. Oh many
times where the creek
        was fiercest where

light broke on the water
        like a knife
entering the eye. That
        shallow lost
creek, those useless kick-
        ing white legs
and no name you could
        ever learn.

The Stone Well

Six feet from the rim the old vertigo begins.
In the tall grass flattened and gone to seed.
In the white glare of the October sun.
In the murmur of insects, in the smell of stone.
What's hunger but a smell of stone.
Come here! Closer.

This is the well so deep there's no bottom.
This is the well your grandfather's father drilled through rock.
This is the well that once had a wooden bucket, and a crank
     to turn, to lower the bucket.
This is the well of the tin roof like a helmet.
This is the well once struck by lightning in a midsummer storm.
This is the well that is an inverted tower into Earth.
This is the well of the family snapshots against which you posed.
This is the well ablaze in sunshine.
This is the well in whose loosened stone garter snakes coil hidden.
This is the well of which you dream when you have no dreams.
This is the well of terror and solace.
This is the well of stammered syllables.
This is the well of memory, and memory's tricks.
This is the well of time crumbling like rock.
This is the well of brackish odors not to be named.
This is the well of oblivion. Your inheritance.
This is the well into which you fall, inconsequential
     as the translucent husk of an insect.
You never did exist.

Five hundred miles, and thirty years.
     "—losing her way—"
     "—well, it was his time—"
     "—heavy-hearted—"
     "—made her peace—"
     "—always loved *you*—his favorite—"
Uncle's voice lifts urgent, quickened by whiskey.

The war in Korea, *his* war. Nobody remembers! Gives a damn!
Starving, dysentery, his weight down to one-thirty, he's
    a walking skeleton. Mud, rats. The siege of Seoul.
    How he'd prayed—*him!* Those fifteen days in solid rain
    driven along the Han River like cattle, the Communists
    killing stragglers with butts of rifles, knives, you died
    in the mud and were left behind like garbage and he'd
    half-carried in his arms a kid from Depew, farm kid
    like himself, wounded in the groin and the flesh bloated,
    festering with maggots.
Jesus, the things I seen...
I mean, you kids...what do you know!
So many times he'd tell his story, the words got worn smooth
    like old coins. The thinnest copper pennies.
(Always in Uncle's story, the kid from Depew survived.
You were twenty years old when a relative said scornfully
no he hadn't, he'd died in the POW camp, and when your uncle
went to see his family, expecting he'd be welcomed, they
hardly invited him inside to sit down, never offered him
a drink, and he never got over it, it's the kid from Depew
he's mad at, telling that pathetic story every time
he gets drunk like there's some point to it? it's maybe going
to turn out different, told another time?)

Your grandfather was the joker of the family.
Grabbing you beneath the arms—how the armpits hurt!—
    carrying you, a child of four or five, to the well
    to toss you in!
Laughing drunk on Four Roses, unshaven, in a good mood.
You know Grandpa loves you, crazy about kids.
Lifting you over the well's rim, legs kicking, you're sobbing
    clutching at the stone, your fingers bleed, nails tear.
Just teasing, you know how he is. Don't be silly.

In the collapsed shed, the 1948 International Harvester
    tractor bought the summer before his death.

To live a life without premeditation.
Without theory.

As far as you dare you lean over the old stone well.
This harsh sunshine dispels memory.
You're all right. You're fine. You're here,
    and in control.
Of course, the well has a bottom. Twenty feet down.
But the water has dried up, now there's a tarry muck.
Thick rotted compost of leaves, tree branches, skeletons
    of mice, birds—
The stink of ancient damp stone.
A glimmer down there of something blue, broken glass?—
    plastic?—incapable of rotting.
Looks like forever.

Marsena Sportsmen's Club, 1957

Girls weren't wanted. Only boys, nine-
and ten-year-olds paid to wring necks briskly,
or twist off heads, when the targets
failed to die. First the gunfire that
makes your head ring then the shrieking and wing-
flapping, little feathery explosions of blood
and pain and some of the pigeons could still fly,
it was amazing how they could still fly,
winding up a mile away in somebody's yard
or crash-diving against a window or in some woman's
laundry hanging on the line so there was hell
to pay, you bet.
25¢ per pigeon seemed like a lot from
the Marsena Sportsmen's Club where none
of our fathers could afford to belong.

Those little kids' hands, smeared with blood—
you knew not to expect mercy, from those hands.

Child Walking in Sleep

Night, and the bright bone moon.
And the snow-slanted roof.
And the timbers of the old house creaking
with cold. And you grind your teeth in sleep
not knowing you sleep. And someone calls.

The covers thrown off, the pale bare blind feet
groping, your eyes are open and sightless
and your head sways on its long stalk,
this is risk, this is danger, the sleepwalker must not
be wakened too suddenly or his heart might stop
but someone calls and you must answer.

Now the cold floorboards now the stairs the rooms subtle
and strange with shadow, the carpet afloat,
a clock chimes but it is a clock in your sleep,
an eye burns white and mad at the window but it is your eye.
Such bliss in sleep not knowing you sleep
not knowing you walk bruising your flesh without pain,
and how without surprise, body
and spirit so powerfully conjoined.
O may you sleep forever in mid-stride!

No one calls that is not you
and one by one those who might wake you will die.
The blue-bright winter morning is hours away.
You are a child walking in sleep in bliss
in a dream that replicates the world blind and wise
and unheeding there, in that house,
that night.

Snapshot Album

Pages to be turned
slowly, to prevent everything
from happening at once.

Why do you think you might go here,
where no one knows you? Here
darkness is never recorded
except by error.
Or sometimes a patch of blinding happy fire pouring
from the sky.

In the oldest of the snapshots
the world is without color, gently
tinted with brown. The album's
inhabitants take no notice, smiling
as if in full color, and alive,
just like you.
It is 1921, it is 1938,
it is 1942, and so swift.

       In one snapshot there's a dark
squirmy child posed on your grandmother's lap
and who holds the camera?—fixing you there
in a dead woman's arms. It is 1942.
So fleshy, warm. That powdery
smell like waking from a dream you begin
to lose even as you wake, sliding away
swift, anonymous.

Undertow, Wolf's Head Lake

These late summer waves break slow, flat, spent,
soothing, the blood's subdued beat,
for instance if you lie in bed
neither asleep nor awake
and you've eased down inside your body
where the heart is no larger
than a baby's fist
barely needing to pulse,
then you remember swimming this lake,
twelve years old, long legs, arms
narrow and hard with muscle,
the breath, the beat,
dusk easing up from below,
frothy craters warmed from a long day's sun,
that giant eel
brushing cold against an ankle,
a leg, the sudden icy caress against the shoulder—
now the current shifts,
now the lazy pocked surface slips away
and you are breathing black water,
snorting, choking,
dusk in the mountains too swift to be believed—
your legs heavy, knees gone numb,
the breath quick and thin
in slivers like glass—

You kick loose, you are swimming away,
overhead a small flock of Canadian geese passes,
the beat, again the beat.
Nothing has touched me, you think, swimming away, as the familiar waves break spent, warm,
flat, sleepy, you rise dripping in shallow water,
toes clawing the sand,
The undertow? you say, *Oh was that the undertow?*

You might have drowned. You lived,
and immediately forgot.
What to make of old surprises, old loves,
broken shells between the toes?
These dull spent late summer waves at Wolf's Head Lake?

And here I am, you say,
here, still, I am.

The Infant's Wake

10 A.M. Saturday, late winter
draining into the gutters.

Fear is palpable as the hissing steam heat.
Vertigo rises from the carpet.
Lilies and white asters, white carnations,
the subtlest of odors.
A casket, white-gleaming, so small a single pallbearer
might bear it away.

Our baby cousin on his altar absorbs the room's light.
It is Death but it cannot be named.
Blossom-pale skin, rosy cheeks,
those tiny perfect features,
a watercolor about to melt.

Wings beat against the windows,
a sudden gusty rain.

There is a fussy authority to those who kneel and pray.
For the rest, vertigo rises from the carpet.
The facts are cardiac arrest, a mother-of-pearl casket,
lacy pillow, lacy nightgown, strange-gripping damp hands.
So good of you to come, thank you for coming,
thank you so much for coming,
it is Death but it cannot be named
nor does the infant, now, retain his name.

It is impossible to speak of the dead infant
except to say No, or Why.
It is impossible to look at that face
and impossible to look away.
The room is a swaying vessel,
adrift at sea.
The light is that of a camera's flashbulb
that will not fade.

If weeping begins there is the danger it will not end.
Still, it begins.
All Saturday drains into the gutters.

Recurring Dream of Childhood

July humid and heavy as spite. The long afternoon waning. You've never been equal
to the love you've been given and to punish
you comes suddenly that dream of the other night

or will it be tonight, the dream like the poem
is silence pried open though when you examine it
closely you see that nearly every detail is wrong—
the faces of your family have the texture of rock

or vapor, the walls dissolve as you approach
into rooms you never knew, all things blurred
or too precise, verging on pain small as a fingernail that becomes the entire body! If the farmhouse

is the house of your childhood then you are the wrong
age to be weeping like mercury spilled across a table
top or your grandfather is already dead but sitting
calmly in the kitchen dropping cigarette ash

onto his work clothes and reading *The Buffalo Evening News*.
Your black Labrador puppy has grown into a strange dog
and who is that sitting hunched his head in his hands
where no lover of yours ever sat in this house

and what is the dream's logic that the staircase
is in the living room. And the stairs steep as night-
mare. And the windows so high. Laughter like steel
wool in your throat but it's your laughter, raw, sur-

prised, or is this weeping again and everyone stares.
Some things are exact though you relive them only in
the dream—the smell of the potato field after rain,
the hay grown rancid in the old barn. But your father

is too short for your height isn't he. Oh God he was always
so tall a man. If the coal bin is still in that corner
of the dark unbreathable cellar and the echo still in
the cistern where you dared to lean in. Your mother, or

is it your grandmother, faces you understand without
being able to see, rummaging through a trunk in the spare room
and it is your duty to assist but your muscles are locked,
helpless, there are sharp words, a taste like pewter. *Here
we've been living,* she tells you without recrimination.
Here, we've kept your life for you to fill.

Flash Flood

Our neighbors' Labrador retriever is a clump
of waste wool bobbing drowned against the barn
now the air is angry as wind-flapping laundry
and all the clocks' hands have stopped for good.

Nails waiting to be ripped from boards
and mud waiting to rise
and ditches to become rivers
and no one guessed!

Heaving water smelling of rust.
And rot. And straw. Drumming
lashing the house like flame
so jubilant you want to open the windows
now the clocks' hands have stopped for good.

     In the morning a new landscape of ponds
and lakes and rushing creeks where there were fields,
or nothing you can remember. And the sun washed
clean. So quickly! And no one guessed
the malice waiting! Even the petals
of your mother's peonies waiting to be ripped
and tossed into the air, or into nothing
you might name.

If to be borne away by the flood is to die
how could death be more buoyant?
—just syllables, straws.

Rise Up, O Men of God

The prayers we'd tried
in the wooden church called
Methodist!—those years.
The foot-pedal organ
I played, shouted hymns
slapping the ceiling
like giant moths dazed
in daylight.
O Men of God, each hour
might have been the last.

Still, rivers glitter-
ing like the Nile
threaded my hot eyelids.
Fourteen years old. Sin
on every side.

I'd felt its pulse early
like the pulse of a baby turtle,
bought at Kresge's for 50¢,
tiny snaky head, china-
blue painted shell, doomed
but I released him one day
in a shallow creek.
Dear God don't let him die was
my small prayer.

Each morning, now, thirty
years later, the eye is larger.
Eventually, they say, it will devour the sky.

Elegy: The Ancestors

Now the long dusk-shadows lift from the tall grass
I'm thinking of the dead past thinking of themselves.
I'm thinking of my maiden great-aunts B___ & E___.
My Grandmother R___ who loved me & I was too young
to know & love in return. I'm thinking of the hump-backed
H___ the hired man—"hired man" is what he was called,
through thirty-six years—found dead at last, frozen
in his shanty New Year's Day 1954 & the shanty stuffed
with newspapers & filth-stiffened clothes & rags in passage-
ways narrow as a hive's. I'm thinking of Grandpa V___
& his heated boxes of quails' eggs in stacks & baby quail
cheeping in his uplifted hands. & my uncle T___ working
the fields like a mule to eat, & eating to work the fields.
Calloused hands snagging in my curls.

They were good lives that mostly came to nothing.
Memory like a cobweb net retains them briefly.
No one has honored them in verse nor even in prose.
The *Ransomville Weekly Gazette* obituary page & of course
their tidy grave markers behind the Lutheran Church speak
of them in familiar terms so even Death is no alarm &
no surprise.

Don't expect solace from me, who's received enough
to know its worth.

The Lord Is My Shepherd I Shall Not Want

In August, in upstate New York,
summer turns sullen.
Blacktop highways sticky as licorice.
Red earth cracked like an old farmer's hands.

One by one they left the high stone house
    of their ancestors.
One by one entering the graveyard tottering
    downhill behind the Ransomville Lutheran Church.

I wasn't one of them, I escaped early.
I never believed.
I don't believe anything anyone has ever told me.
I wouldn't believe even you if you swore to me
    the deepest truth of your tinsel heart.

Nostalgia

Rural District School #7, Ransomville, New York

Crumbling stone steps of the old schoolhouse
Boarded-up windows   shards of winking glass
Built 1898, numerals faint in stone as shadow
Through a window, obedient rows of desks   mute
Only a droning of hornets beneath the eaves,
the cries of red-winged blackbirds by the creek

How many generations of this rocky countryside grown & gone
How many memories   & all forgotten
no one to chronicle, no regret

& the schoolhouse soon to be razed   & goodbye America
The flagless pole, what relief!
I love it, the eye lifting skyward   to nothing
Never to pledge allegiance to the United States of America
     again
Never to press my flat right hand over my heart again
     as if I had one

III

What Is Most American
Is Most in Motion

$

If you have it you don't think about it
so acquiring it is the means of forgetting it
because if you don't have it you'll think about it
and you're embittered thinking about it because
to think about it is to acknowledge yourself
incomplete without it because you know you are
superior to the many who have it thus need never
think about it the way, after Death,
you won't think about Death either.

Orion

"Never doubt me.
How can you doubt me?"

Bodies naked and squirmy
as phosphorescent fish.
That drunken slant to the horizon,
goofy perspective,
cheap starlight through the windows...
the rooms in which we met were dreams
poorly solidified around the dreamer.

Yet, those hot frantic afternoons!
Those years. Collapsed
like a child's balloon.
I trusted you, and you lied,
and I forgave you.

Clockwork Orion rolling through our bones.
You'll pay. You'll pay.

Recollection, in Tranquility

He ran his hard hands over me like Braille,
he liked to bruise the skin of breasts, ribcage.
"Why are you so thin?" he asked.
My body a rebuke to his stern solid flesh.

What's the effort of love but a kind of swimming
through another's flesh?
A man's need, so sudden & hot!
It's intimidating no matter how many times
it's happened in just the same way.

It's faces that love, we know that.
We know better, but we know that.
Mine was covered in a porcelain shell of which I think
I was vain: large liquid-empty eyes, polite mouth,
skin without history.
Beneath that face, the other he never saw.
Contorted in strain, in hope, in anger.
Female passion that's sheerly muscle,
mouth like a pike's.

He saw the one, spoke and pleaded with the one,
those eyes, that mouth, but the other, beneath,
he never knew, nor guessed.
What worried him was—"Sometimes I think I might kill you."

In the end nothing came of it.
We remained married to other people. We grew older.

Insomnia

Lie down in sleep but suddenly
this windowless bathroom?
white-glaring tiles? porcelain
sink so fiercely scoured
it's dancing with flames?
and no shadowy corners?
and the chrome faucets
too hot to touch? and
the perfect pool of the toilet
bowl in which a single eyeball
floats? and the mirror
so polished there's nothing
beyond the surface not even
                    you?

He Was Talking About His Friend

He was talking about his friend
who'd died of cancer, a famous writer
at the end, and much-loved. But he'd died.
And this man's courage, dying young;
his public nobility;
the way he'd grip our hands, and
kiss our cheeks;
the warmth of his touch, his smile—
Hey. It's O.K. I don't mind. I'm fine.

This was a New York editor talking about his friend
who'd been his writer too, and so he knew.
Now leaning forward, a sombre look,
eyes damp with regret, saying,
"But, in private, he was a different man.
He didn't want to die. He was terrified of—
what was coming." A pause. Lowered voice.
"At the end, you'd have to say
he'd gone a little crazy."
And silence fell upon the dinner table, nine faces
rapt, prurient, scared.

Every friend's a son of a bitch,
in the end. Can you doubt it?

Hands, Prints, Time: A Collage

> The landscape that he was looking at
> recurred so often in his dreams he was never
> fully certain whether or not he was seeing it
> in the real world.
> —George Orwell, *1984*

Don't delude yourself, you too will surrender
both hands to the State.
Only wait.

*

Each fingerprint *is* unique.
Like snowflakes, and flies.
Like faces. And, like faces,
they age, they wear away.

*

Said the moustached police officer, some people
you just can't get good prints off of,
it's their field of work like for instance
a bank clerk—all that paper money,
smooths out your prints, pretty fast.
But we have other means
of identification.

*

"I watch people's hands now,
like when they're talking, and gesturing,
or if they're, like, sitting alone,
and don't know anybody's watching.
Hands don't know how to lie."

*

On the platform before the smiling strangers
I smiled, and proceeded to unravel my guts

hand over hand, like silky yarn. There was applause,
and I wound them back together, and more applause,
and I stepped down.

*

Did you ever feel your hands fly? leap into life?
Snowy February afternoons, here alone
I'd sit at the piano as at a shrine, and surrender
to playing Bach: Three-Part Inventions
pencil-annotated thirty-five years ago
and all the notes forgotten except
in my astonishing fingers, where
I can't enter.

*

"Three things Daddy used to say:
shake hands looking a man direct in the eye,
keep your life pure and simple,
—and the third, I forget."

*

"Uncle Jon-Jon used to say one body
and one pair of hands wasn't enough for him
which is why, we guess, he ended up
weighing three hundred pounds."

*

Now nobody runs his hard hands over me, as if
measuring the skeleton beneath the skin,
I've lost the capacity to see myself.

*

The moustached police officer took my hands
in his, pressing each fingertip, in turn, onto
the inked pad, and then onto the pad
of clean white paper, where, like incriminating
dreams in daylight, miniature faces appeared!

These are the minutes that, made into records,
are guaranteed to outlive us all.

*

"It began with my hands. Just happened
to notice, one day—the backs, the veins
bulging, and ropy-like, and the skin kind of wrinkled
like an old glove, and what I'd thought were moles
or freckles, spreading. And from my hands it spread
to my face, and it seemed to go quick.
And now I'm what you'd have to call *old.*"

*

Aborted, it turned out to be eyeless, and
noseless, and lacking what would have been
a normal digestive tract. But there
were the miniature hands: fingers,
fingernails, fingerprints.

Upstairs

Babe lumbering on her fleshy heels,
Jimbo cracking her across the mouth.
The radio blares, it is Saturday.
He slammed me then I slammed him.
To turn the other cheek was great.
To be struck like that, to force
his muscle!—
You don't know what it's like to be loved!
Clawing blood down his cheek,
everything hot and rich in my mouth.

Downstairs from upstairs
the shouts get swallowed in rock music.
Her breathy screams,
bare feet.
Is this why we are born, you wonder.
You hunch in a corner and wonder.

There Was a Shot

and then silence, except for screams he didn't hear
since he was concentrating on walking, and,
walking, he knew not to falter in his stride since
momentum carries us forward, and not logic,
nor even strength.

He was crossing West Huron, the traffic lights were swaying,
and he was too distracted to notice the trickling down
his legs, warm, and sudden, and shameful as urine,
his socks and his shoes are already soaked, a wild
itching in his gut, his bellybutton aflame.

He was in motion, he was aware that that's the trick,
not to stumble at the curb like a drunk, though the curb
is higher than he'd expected, and West Huron wider, O God
now's not the time to hesitate, nor even to glance down
to what's dragging at his feet.

He was waxy in the face, he was using his arms as paddles,
he was floating, he was sinking, he was ignoring the red
splotches on the pavement like coins falling from his pockets,
he was three blocks from home and didn't know his name
and he was preparing to laugh it off, and even forgive.

He was ignoring the faces, and he wasn't hearing the voices,
and when we touched him he wrenched away, the trick is just
to move one foot in front of the other, that's the primary trick
from which all others follow, not to falter, not to break
your stride, not to glance down, oh never.

What's a wild shot on a Saturday night, a stray bullet
from a skidding car, what's *accident*, but nobody's at fault,
make the best of a bad thing he knew so he was telling
this story to anybody willing to listen, once he got to
where he was going, and they knew him.

The Black Glove: A Rapture

> Hide your God. He's your strength.
> —Paul Valéry

I looked up to see an object falling from a high window
    like a shot bird!—
and there on the sidewalk at my feet lay the black glove—
splay-fingered, faint tincture of blood,
life twitching from it, and gone.

*

A mongrel dog trotted across the street bearing the black glove
    in its teeth.

*

Next, amid a display of expensive leather gloves behind
    the shop window—
the single black glove.

*

The black glove, filthy, a finger missing, amid pigeon
    droppings,
on the base of the war monument.

*

The woman's fingers in the black glove, slowly
    caressing her throat.
Barely seen through the tinted windows of the idling Jaguar
    this gold-spangled October afternoon.
O love!—but I neither know your name nor can see your face,
    only the black glove, caressing.

*

The streets were lined with helmeted policemen.
The protesters marched twelve abreast.
Men, women. Pale angry faces. The sepia glaze of history.

61

The banners they carried were soaked in rain, the heavy folds
    of cloth obscuring the names of their towns, origins.
The wind rose, blowing rain aslant across the pavement.
Across the avenue, past the marchers' feet, the black glove
    flew, unobserved.

                            *

The black glove smelling of cold.
The black glove shoved into your overcoat pocket.
The black glove beneath the hotel bed, a disembodied hand.
On the tile windowsill of the restaurant, the black glove
    creeping like a rat.

                            *

The messenger wearing one black glove on his skeletal right hand—
    in the light cast outward through our doorway,
    warm-cozy-tender light of long marriage,
    teeth smiling and the delivery of the packet *for you*
    and *for you.*

                            *

"Shit, man, I don't know, how'm I gonna know. Ain't given
    to us, ignorant as we is, to *know.*
Like this glove I'm wearing?—I see it on the bench there,
I put it on, it's mine.
Might be, it's always been mine.
No big deal, man, but how're you gonna *know?*"

American Holiday

Military New Year's Eve!
Jets bombarding the sky with confetti!
Heroes' welcome-homecoming
plummeting out of the sky!

Bugles brassy with being right,
flares reddening peasant hills!

After the first of the explosions
thousands of unidentified birds scattered skyward.
The air darkened with shrieks.
Here below our nostrils were impacted
with hair, or wet ashes.

Only Monday.
A long week ahead.

Like Walking to the Drug Store, When I Get Out

Dear Joyce Carol—

This is the 5th time for me to be writing to you
& I promise it is the last.
I know your reading this Joyce Carol
but I cant prove it can I!

I saw your picture in the paper here.
Maybe you were in Iowa City.
I told you I have a story to tell you
you could write up but you let that opportunity pass.
That's tough shit for you Joyce Carol
only one day you'll know how much.

I'm locked up here for child molestation.
I wont tell you whether I'm guilty or innocent
on account of I've already done 6½ yrs
& guilt or innocence doesnt matter to me now.
I know your asking do you have remorse,
well remorse for what?
Do YOU have remorse?

You people have done everything you want
to me, doesn't that give me equal right.
If you spit in my face & insult me & throw me in solitary
what do you think you will be repaid
when I get out of here?

Look, I never did anything I'd feel guilty about.
I wouldn't do anything I'm ashamed of.
You don't know me, Joyce Carol but thats not my nature.
If youd taken down my story then youd know.
But you wouldnt give me shit & now it's too late.
Maybe I haven't done enough, maybe
that's what I'm ashamed of.

Maybe I should have killed four or five hundred people!
I think now I would feel better.
When I had the chance, but now I don't.
Then I would know I really offered society something!
I'd know I made my mark, like you.
If I wanted to kill somebody
I'd just grab a baseball bat and I'd beat you
till your brains leaked out.
& I wouldn't feel a thing.
I'd be just like walking to the drug store, when I get out.

What do you want to call me a child molester for?
I never molested anyone.
I don't need to molest anyone.
You capitalist swine are molesting your own sons & daughters
& the Constitution condones every bit of it!
In my whole life I burglarized a 7–11, some nickels & dimes
& busted open a stamp machine
& some cars & cashed a couple checks.
All of which shit I was never caught for & thus
no record of proof available.

I am not a child molester.
I like pussy with hair on it.
Lots of hair on it.
I saw your picture in the paper & your too old for me.
Believe me if I started murdering people
there'd be none of you left.

PS. The U.S. started World War II.

Ballad of Ashfield Avenue

Along Ashfield Avenue connecting with I-75, rain
falls like steel filings. The air's gassy gauze. Are all
   these neighborhoods so wasted? Driving to hit
the green lights. Scared shitless you're gonna hit red.
   And sit in your Saab sedan, doors locked, eyes straight
staring ahead. *Get me the hell out of here O Lord,*
   never be wicked again.

Along Ashfield Avenue, man, think we can't track
your pulp-paper face? Scared eyes noting shut-down stores,
   burnt-out Kroger's? Vacant lots gone to jungle,
and the *stink!* Like burning tires, backed-up drains.
   You're thinking *If this is how these people choose*
to live. Thinking *If they want to burn their own neighborhoods,*
   live like animals for Christ's sake!

Pisses you, you voted Democrat. Always have. You
a *good soul.* We know. That heart-glow you felt Christmas 1979
   tossing a quarter in my bucket at the Airport Hilton,
good Christian feeling *giving to the poor & needy* long as
   you don't see us or breathe the same air. Long as
you hit the green lights, north to I-75. *Hey lemme clean*
   your windshield, man? No?

Or you could gimme a little blood?

'Course I'm jivin, man! No need to panic. Can't trust
none of these niggers but I'm the exception. Parole's over
   now I'm in rehab. Next comes *job training.* You American
you put your faith in *job training.* See me hauling your trash
   that's *city sanitation worker.* Carrying your dirty plates
that's *bus boy.* Minimum wage a victory for the underclass,
   man we're *grateful.* HIV-positive but *grateful.*

So you could gimme a little blood?

My sad daddy (now deceased) worked the heavy mower
at the edge of the Great Books you teach, you'd look out
    your mullioned windows pissed at the noise. Didn't make
the Great Books, broke his back laying cement for Centenary
    Hall. All I want's a little blood, *trans-fus-ion.* Cau-
casian-pure, 100% American blood shining red like liquid
    Formica. You got plenty to spare.

    Ain't you prime health? Like the President that's *fit,*
tanned and rested after every vacation? Spirit of optimism
    is required. Every house in Lakepointe "sensory-wired"
and SWAT-teams on 24-hour alert. You looking at me not see-
    ing me, hell that's O.K. Thinking weird thoughts
about me not knowing me, I ain't complaining. Writing
your shit about me. *'Course I'm jivin.* I'm in the street
    waving my stump arms hey it's O.K. *I don't exist.*

    Blood don't cost. Anyway ain't you in-sured?
On I-75 in this bad rain so the underpass is flooded
    and the Saab stalls and I'm the six-foot baby-face kid
grinning in your window. Yo, man! You needin some help?
    Banging the glass with my tire iron. And
you're saying, Look it wasn't me! I'm not my skin! No more
    than you! Wasn't my fault any of it don't hurt *me!*
It's a misunderstanding, look at history but not *me!*
    And I'm laughing, O.K., man! Cool. Nobody
gonna hurt you, just gimme a little blood.

What Is Most American Is Most in Motion

What is most American is most in motion!
Driving all day, luxury of the sky,
CONSTRUCTION AHEAD and RESUME NORMAL SPEED and
all pain of memory, because all memory,
behind. And we're in love, in America,
though we should not boast, for such stirs
envy like big tarnished spoons in hearts
as American as ours, and as muscled.

No one needs to remind us RESUME NORMAL SPEED
on the interstate splendid as an Ionic column
laid flat upon the continent among vertical
plunges of telephone poles, Kansas granaries,
K-Mart parking lots like enormous dance floors
no one has seen as they deserve. And
corporate headquarters flanked by thousands
of fat Canada geese! and those exquisite small ponds
false as mirrors, and as irresistible!

In Bea's Diner in Orion, Kansas, an elderly gentleman
tells me, "To find a thing beautiful may be just a way
of saying you've found a thing." As RESUME NORMAL
SPEED draws us forward into the next time
zone, and the next. Euclidean propositions
of smokestacks, trashed autohulks, great American
diesels whose motors never sleep—what is this
continent, and who has seen it whole?

WARNING CONSTRUCTION AHEAD but we're bearing west
sporty as these yellow bulldozers grinding what's left
of what's here and hungry, like us, for more.
RESUME NORMAL SPEED because no pain of memory and no
gauge except the gas needle's red and now suddenly
what's this?—Quincy, Nebraska with white First Lutheran
Church and spire, Meridian County Courthouse with clock
tower backlit at sunset like a psychedelic candy box cover,
crimson satin you want to run your big thumb over,
and over.

Dakota Mystery, 10 May 1994

Above North Dakota seeing the ghastly dun-colored earth
    flat & dissolving into the horizon like expelled breath
descending, Northwest flight 151,
    Minneapolis to Fargo, wind buffeting the plane &
below, rising in rectangles—"property"—
    farmland bounded by roads ruler-straight & absurd
each rectangle interchangeable with all others
    horror of mud-rivers, leafless trees
& the sky bleached out, *gone*

The emptiness inside the atom: here

Swiftly descending, the shadow seeping out of the earth
    rising to meet us & swallow us
& terror like a fork striking glass
    the fine crystalline vibration
too subtle to shatter glass ringing in our ears

        As we file out of the plane a voice calls out
        Is this the eclipse?
        & another voice replies, cheerful matter-of-fact
        That was the eclipse. It's all over.

Frequent Flier I

In the sky's blue eye distance draws
like a magnet.

Clouds like syllables of sheer ecstasy
and even the blue is fake,
as you've been told.

Here?—where you weren't
just now. And where
you won't be,
soon.

In the time it takes you to read these lines.
In the time it takes you to turn
a page, or smile out the window
at what's rushing, there,
unnamed and of absolutely no consequence,
in the sky's blue eye.

Frequent Flier II

Anyone who plunges into infinity, in both time and place, farther and farther without stopping, needs fixed points, mileposts as he flashes by, for otherwise his movement is indistinguishable from standing still.
—Escher

How delicious, to step into this new skin!
At Newark International Airport at 7:49 A.M. my heels winged
    like Mercury gliding the walkway!
Disembodied angel-voices *Dallas-Ft. Worth! Miami!*
    Cincinnati! Las Vegas!
A sun-spangled cloudless morning, good!
A morning opening into eternity, what joy!
What ecstasy, to fling my life like dice!
In my new skin, my radiant eyes & springy step!
Invisible & anonymous, what romance!
At Continental Gate 22 my heart quickens: FLIGHT DEPARTS
    ON TIME!
First-Class passengers may now board!
How delicious snugly belted in (window)seat 2A!
& already diet Sprite in a plastic cup is proffered,
I am made to feel royal & welcome!
Now on the runway bump-bumping like a child's wagon!
Flight attendants prepare for take-off!
Be sure belts buckled & luggage safely stowed!
Airborne abruptly veering upward & the runway falling away!
At 30,000 feet *our cruising height* breakfast is served!
Veering westward to Chicago? Denver? Phoenix?
Clouds break & hiss about the wings' silvery span!
How delicious, to abandon myself to oblivion & flaming
    wreckage!
What a royal breakfast of linen napkins, "glass" glasses,
    choice of omelette or cereal & fruit! in a vase a single
    flower of indeterminate species!
Why will you say the air is too thin to bear our weight?
Why will you say the air is invisible, is soul invisible?

Why will you say it is vanity & madness to step off the ground?
Did not Daedalus step off the ground, did not Daedalus brave
    the sun?
It's an ordinary morning & an ordinary flight, even in my new
    skin that's a fact I must acknowledge!
I've been here before, I meet myself returning swaying from
    the lavatory, I avoid my eyes!
Through the pressurized cabin waft the usual psittacosis viruses,
    Bacillus leprae, airborne TB!
Belted snug in seat 2B my faceless companion reads *Forbes,*
I am belted snug at 30,000 feet reading *Scientific American!*
Must mark off universe into units of a certain length I am reading!
Infinity within a geometric figure I am reading!
En route to Washington, D.C., or is it Denver, the surprise
    of an elegant luncheon!
Linen napkins! "glass" glasses! cocktail shrimp, sesame hard
    roll, *coq au vin!*
Red wine, white wine! in carafes! Swiss chocolate mints & each
    mint costing only $40!
In the corner of my eye I see the first flames leap!
I hear the engines coughing gravel!
Saying nothing to my companion in 2B not wishing to raise
    alarm!
I am studying the visual paradoxes of M.C. Escher!
I am reading of the self-reproducing inflationary universe
    inventing & re-inventing itself for eternity!
I am learning that while *here* I am already *not-here!*
I am learning to be stoic & good-humored though *posthumous!*
O let us not crash O God!
Let us not die a communal fiery death in a Nebraska cereal field!
Or, if it's time & fate, let us die in an eye's wink!
No time for remorse, conscience! No time to tear at the plastic
    phone in the armrest beside me! *Goodbye, goodbye, I loved
    you all, why didn't you love me!*
The outline of my spiraling flaming figure defines the empty
    universe that surrounds it!
The cry caught in my throat defines the silence that surrounds it!
The pilot's voice crackles warning of *turbulence ahead!*
Boiling steel-colored clouds & mammoth-husks of vapor!

O corporate America plunging into a sea the hue of fresh-
    minted treasury bills!
Dwarf pillows hurriedly passed out, & blankets!
Why will you say that airplane dreams are thin & unsatisfying
    as suet?
Waking dazed! clouds beneath the plane delicate & pinkly
    rippled as the roof of a cat's mouth!
Is this a pleat in time into another day,
is the cryptogram 30,000 feet below oblivious of our shadow
    passing over!
What evidence of civilization there, *intelligent life!*
"Interstate highways"—"railroads"—"urban centers"!
They had a gift, *Homo sapiens,* for infinite repetition!
They had a gift, *Homo sapiens,* for grids! horizontal/vertical
    planes!
Afflicted with hunger, *Homo sapiens,* for ceaseless motion!
Strapped into my seat forty minutes from Seattle where *airport
    visibility* is poor!
No: a holding pattern above Buffalo, headwinds at 60 miles per
    hour! Rain turning to sleet!
Unable to land at Kennedy, veering southward to Philly!
Why do we love our ridiculous lives, do we imagine they are *us?*
Do we imagine *martyrdom* in a blank sky!
Seat belts fastened! Tray tables in upright position!
Drunken winds & the plane bears its cargo courageously!
Lights flicker like brain cells! The air in the cabin is stale
    as many exhaled breaths!
We are going to plummet & die, our anonymous hearts lurch as
    one!
Fifty-five minutes circling the fogbound airport through clouds
    dense as pond algae!
The heart's lurch as the wing's wheels emerge!
Flight attendants prepare for landing!
Something rises in a swoon to meet us! Darkness winking
    with fibrillating lights!
In the parallel universe *The plane seemed to flip at landing & burst
    into a giant fireball! to the absolute astonishment of witnesses!*
    but no: the plane's wheels are bumping along the runway,
    we're here, we've landed! At last!

Who would wish to live in any other universe, when
     you think of it?
Whoever among us prayed for a fiery oblivion, we have survived
     just the same!
Another happy landing!
None of us ever doubted,
we break into spontaneous applause!

Why will you say there is no romance in a late arrival,
11:18 P.M. the head aching & throat parched at Newark
     International Airport?
The concourse near-deserted & semi-darkened, a vacuum cleaner
     sullenly droning!
Five worried-looking strangers waiting for loved ones at the gate,
     tearful hugs & kisses! & none for me!
Yet how delicious, *I am on the ground!*
What joy thrumming my veins, *I am on the ground!*
Sighting five crew members from the flight, tall pilot & co-pilot
     & three young women attendants all in stylish uniform
     pulling their luggage behind them!
What are they murmuring together, laughing? Just out of earshot?
I observe them striding away tall & indifferent as demigods
     past shuttered newsstands, darkened PASTA & PIZZA &
     I CAN'T BELIEVE IT'S YOGURT!
I follow close behind them now floating above them twisted
     in speechless yearning like the husband floating above
     his wife in Chagall's "The Kiss"!

IV

In the Country of the Blue

The Riddle

One morning the package arrives in the mail.
Your name, your address. In an almost familiar hand.
Mailed in 1971 and forwarded many times.
Stamped RECEIVED IN DAMAGED CONDITION U.S. POST OFFICE.

For long hours you contemplate the package.
The handwriting. The triple row of faded stamps.
Yards of fraying twine and yellowed adhesive tape
wound tight as strangulation.

You measure the package with your arms, it's a fit.

You contemplate the package but do not open it.
You tell yourself you are not frightened.
You tell yourself *When it's time.*
You are simply postponing the adventure of—
when it's time.

Motive, Metaphor

Rain
black-dripping
for hours, days
so I hid, here.
This tight cage.
The words are bars
that confine but
there I'd drown.
Did.

Burning Oak, November

Yesterday, the sky in mute
horizontal swaths. Air
too thick to breathe.
Indignant we found the stump
of an aged oak, man-

sized. Burning without flame
at the edge of a clearing. Raw
splintered wood, bulldozed roots exposed
like nerves white in terror.

Even the black soldier-ants fled
such a stench of aged grief
made public and final, all hope exposed—
past tense! Now headless leafless
just a stump knocked
half out of the earth

and the soul merely blue smoke vague
slow-spreading like poison in water
rising without grace or urgency
into a weekday sky no one will paint
or photograph, or see—
except the two of us.
Yesterday.

The Insomniac

Fearful of what was inside carefully she painted
a face upon her face.

Joy threatens?—run bathwater scalding to fill
all allotted space with steam.

Mid-night, when the constellations veer
like drunken vehicles, and no one's to see!

And impossible to locate any horizon—
the cure for motion sickness.

What has been this life? the rusted shears inquire
hanging from a spike in the barn.

This life? your life? wind like a panicked creature
swimming the shoulder-high reeds.

Night rises in a vertical plane.
Day languorous flattened waves, a tepid wash,
horizontal. Barely wetting your shoes.

The insomniac prays to pillow and head
in impossible conjunction.

The insomniac would breathe goose-feather down
if that would resolve his condition.

The insomniac awaits lucidity when the first
of the harsh happy jays sing.

The question posed solely at night *What is this life,
your life, and why* dispelled briskly by morning news.

Yet must have slept for minutes waking stunned,
already smiling at the raw young wind at every window?

Exactly, almost, as before.

Old Concord Cemetery

Gravity rises like mist from the earth.
The solace of old death.
Implausibly regimented rows
of grave markers thin as skeletal hands
translucent as this morning's sky.

Yet not silence but the muttering
of traffic for beyond death there is
traffic, old death is always bounded by
traffic, the oldest here *Thomas Hartshorn d. 1697*
about whom nothing more is known.

Cemetery solitude, amid carbon monoxide.
Mossy companionable earth. With relief
you guess *the present can be born nobly*
as the past, it's over so quickly.

Summer Squall, Monhegan Island

By noon the air is crazed with water.
The sea is all sky.
Rags of rain clouds rushing ground-level
as locomotives. Shreds, bits of pottery,
white-bearded lunacy and no harm to butchery!—
the squall!

The squall! the squall! urging you to recall
why you'd come here, such
distance as if *There must be purpose*
if we've come so far.
The squall!

And abruptly then blown away, aside,
a shrug of the sky, gale-gusts fiery
out of the east and that sudden yawning sun.
And all's quiet again, almost.
Exactly, almost, as before.

Hermit Crab

Legend,
or mere gossip?—
the crab
that, homeless,
appropriates
the shells of creatures
who have died
and rotted away.
"Isn't it ignoble,"
the crab is asked,
"to have no shell,
no defining structure,
of your own?"

"All shells,
all structures,
define"—
the crab's
dignified reply.

(And this too
is an appropriated
cadence.)

George Bellows' "Mrs. T. in Cream Silk, No. 1" (1919–23)

Time?—teaches us.
Time?—chastens us.
Time?—caresses us.
Time?—chisels us.
Time?—erodes us.
Time?—exposes us.
Time?—discloses us.
Time?—prepares us.
Time?—nourishes us.
Time?—catechises us.
Time?—betrays us.
Time?—mythologizes us.
Time?—devours us
        in the name of Wisdom.

The Triumph of Gravity

Dogwood blossoms, pink linen napkins, luncheon
lasting past three o'clock.
Professor of Physics, Emeritus, sits erect
in his wheelchair and amuses the table
with spacetime novelties...
trapped light, closed time, "singularities,"
the eventual Triumph of Gravity.

It is everything we have feared,
poetry guesses the worst and is never wrong.
The Universe is finite in volume yet lacks an edge,
space is rubber that bends,
time is a confusion of surfaces,
gravity *merely* geometry,
the pencil point in the heart.

Your body, Joyce Carol, like any star, yearns to shrink
to infinite density and stop time itself by disappearing:
impossible? a miracle? yet it happens.
Yes it is the black hole identified by Wheeler
and vulgarized by many others
but only gravity in different guises.
The sun...and the sun's precise center...and your own
body of liquids and chalky bone.
Thus says Professor, smiling, pale skull filmy with hair,
skin baby-fresh and pink.

When we are leaving Professor shakes hands briskly,
wants to rise but cannot, murmurs smiling, half-angry,
Please forgive,—the shrunken body contending
with its collapsible aluminum chair.

Immobility Defense

First, you run! Fly!
Turn yourself inside-out!
Another time you escape.

Unless this is the time
you don't escape.

*

Well, rend the air with noise!
Screech, squeal, squawk, scream.
You're equipped, use it, hurry!
Bleat, cry. Caterwaul.
Confuse your pursuer!
Flap, flail, flutter, beat your wings!
Your gills fibrillate oxygen.
You burrow into luscious black muck.
Hide in that thicket, like debris.
Fly into the nearest tree.
Plunge head-on into a hole.

You may run farther if there is a farther.

Unless this is the time you don't.

*

Are your feathers not exquisite camouflage in the open field?
Is your fur not exquisite camouflage in the shadowed forest?
Is your speckled hide not exquisite camouflage in the speckled sun?

Until this time.
This final time.

When unexpectedly there's—quiet.
In the grip of jaws—quiet.
You freeze. Gone dreaming.
Your rapid heartbeat slows.
Such beauty in stillness!
Your glazing eyes turn inward, *I'm rethinking this all.*

For what has been *life?*
Appetite, terror, mating. Sleep
and appetite, terror, mating. Sleep
and now pain?
You don't feel it.
Your brain is shutting down like a blackboard being washed clean.
Your heart continues to beat. Gently.
Your blood continues to pulse but not hotly.
Your nerves gone loose, cottony as string.

Whatever these teeth devouring you alive,
you seem almost to welcome them.
Hiding in your body
until your body's gone into the Other.

Such peace I never dreamt.
Until this time.

To an Aged Cat Dying in My Arms

All the solace I can offer,
now you're deaf, blind, trembling
and your breath shuddering,
is my touch—from which,
already stiffening, you begin to shrink.

I Am Krishna, Destroyer of Worlds

Another Monday morning!
At 30,000 feet hurtled through the "sky"!
What does it mean to dwell among strangers
with whom we would not wish to die?

Such Beauty!

Through the night that thin sifting sound
and by morning the world's locked in ice:
a galaxy of ice-petal leaves,
all trees Ionic columns of light.

Such beauty looks permanent, doesn't it?

In the Country of the Blue

However many ways there are of being alive,
it is certain that there are vastly more
ways of being dead, or rather not alive.
—Richard Dawkins, *The Blind Watchmaker*

Walls no more vertical than these
and air of precisely this composition.

A long way down—no ceiling and no floor.
Fierce little gales contend.
Your eyes surrender their vision.

(The heart is not monitored here,
the engine has been disconnected.)

Free fall past vertical cliffs,
where cries echo weirdly.
It is always C-sharp.
It is always present tense.
Except the blue isn't *blue*—
as you'd been warned.

If you were happy there you are happy here.
Though no daylilies bloom bearing their beauty
like freckles, and the smell of wet wool and rubber
in a childhood closet
never pierces the heart.

Those who loved you, whom you'd loved
and might have wished to die for,
had it come to that—their names?
Their faces? Their touch?

It is silence here, it is peace.
All you imagined you craved.

It *is* blue, blown in fierce little gusts.